Bob Ross Bio Painting the World and Story of Bob Ross

"The secret to doing anything is believing that you can do it. Anything that you believe you can do strong enough, you can do. Anything. As long as you believe."

- Bob Ross -

By Chris Michael Hoyt

TABLE OF CONTENTS

INTRODUCTION

As he pauses with a brush on the surface of the canvas, the image already appears to be a gorgeous landscape painting that would look at home in any home. Yet it had only been 15 minutes, and he loved to add trees. The fan brush glides quickly across the canvas while he softly speaks about the tree he is making. Before he gets too far down the canvas, there is a gentle expression of regret; he should have used a larger brush to finish the great tree faster. He is astounded at the magnitude of the large tree as he proceeds down the canvas. As he nears the end, he emphasizes that a larger brush could have produced the same results, albeit a little faster.

Anybody who has seen Bob Ross paint knows that it was unusual for him to include just one tree. This painter thought that everyone should have a buddy around, and this belief extended to all aspects of his work. The second tree takes much less time to appear. It is not only smaller than the massive tree dominating the painting's left side, but it is also partially hidden behind the large tree. He not only painted a fantastic painting in a short period of time, but he also talked about the colors on the palette, the brushes he used, one of his students, his pocket squirrel, and his aim to ensure that everyone has a friend. Most importantly, he's already informed his audience that while working with him, there are no mistakes, only "happy little accidents." His enormous tree appears to fall into this category, as it took him longer to finish than he had anticipated.

As the trees are finished, he starts constructing a small bush, then another, even naming the second one. This emphasizes what he mentioned a few minutes ago: the canvas is yours. You can design any universe you desire on the canvas, adapting and changing it to include an unintentional stroke, misplaced item, or colors you didn't plan to add. All of these alleged flaws can result in a fascinating work of art. He was continually working to dispel the notion that something is a mistake, instead advocating for a painting that may be much better than what was initially intended.

By the time he finished the painting, he had mentioned taking out the trash, how bad he was at fishing, and how he justified adding a trail in the picture to avoid mosquito bites. He emphasized how he lived in the worlds he created, which was why his paintings were always one-of-a-kind; they mirrored his own experiences and interests. It took 30 minutes to make a piece of art that people would want to display in their homes. Instead of selling these idyllic visions from his head, he encouraged people to create their own, implying that he didn't think his paintings were any better than anyone else's.

This gentle encouragement kept people coming back to watch him, not only developing an audience, but also leaving a legacy that has lasted decades beyond his death. Many watch him as much to admire his artistic ability as to create their own paintings, with many viewers having no desire to create their own. Others waited for his soothing voice to keep them company. But, in 2020, his popularity skyrocketed as people were stuck in their houses, crushed by a sense of uncertainty when COVID-19 caused the world to shut down. Suddenly, the man who had discreetly supported people from the 1980s to the mid-1990s was back, but this time he was assisting people in navigating an extremely uncertain period.

Chapter 1:
Early Life

"Don't forget to make all these little things individuals — all of them special in their own way."

Ollie Ross gave birth to Robert Norman Ross at Daytona Beach, Florida on October 29, 1942. This occurred shortly before the United States entered World War Two, and less than two months before the Japanese attack on Pearl Harbor. The family only lived in the area for a brief time before moving to Orlando, Florida, which is around two hours away from where Robert was born. His father, Jack Ross, worked as a carpenter and found work in Orlando. Nonetheless, it is unclear whether this was the reason for the family's relocation. Ross grew up quite quiet, preferring to limit what people knew about him to facts gleaned during his 30-minute television show rather than spending much time being interviewed. The press mainly ignored him, most likely because the people who enjoyed watching his shows didn't watch him due to his personal life. Whatever indications of his background he discussed on the broadcast were, for the most part, more than enough for those who tuned in. As a result, little is known about his childhood.

Details regarding his early childhood are scant because he chose to keep his private life mostly to himself. Ross enjoyed nature, which was one of the few details that became evident after seeing him on the show. His mother was the fundamental source of his respect and passion for animals. Throughout his time on television, he brought animals to show the public that many creatures had been hurt or needed to be rescued, and he was assisting in their recovery. His passion in caring for and healing animals began when he was a child. His love of animals and outdoors was most likely impacted by his 20-year stay in Alaska. Ross mentioned his love of fishing in one of his episodes. Nonetheless, he did not appear to be interested in fishing for food or as a recreation. With a lake visible in the painting, he stated that if he were in that location, he would go fishing. Then he admitted, "I like to fish, but I'm not a very good fisherman. I catch the little fish, then carefully take the hook out of his mouth. Put a band-aid on him, little CPR. Pat him on the too-too, put him back in the water. Go back and catch him again another day." The story wasn't true, but it fits with his love of animals. Ross adopted animals from the show. Some even claimed that he had maintained some unusual pets. Alligators and armadillos were allegedly among the most interesting animals he kept in his home. He appears to be assisting them because these creatures are endemic to Florida and are frequently hit by vehicles or suffer other injuries. That must have been much simpler on his family later in life when the animals that lived with them were significantly less potentially harmful than alligators. Later in life, he was most connected with his pet gray squirrel, who occasionally accompanied him on the show. During one of these visits, he told his audience, "If we're going to have animals around, we all ought to be concerned about them and take care of them."

Ross apparently dropped out of high school during his first year or shortly after finishing the grade. This was the first time he took on a more artistic career, working with his father in the workshop to learn how to be a carpenter. Ross hadn't been in the shop long when an accident severed the top of one of his left hand's fingers. Although it was only the tip of his index finger, it was a terrible loss for someone so young, and he was highly aware of it for the rest of his life. During his shows, it's difficult to notice his damaged finger since he skillfully arranges his palette so that the injury isn't apparent on camera. Following the accident, he realized that a career as a carpenter was not for him. When Ross was 18, he made a decision that would shape the rest of his life: he joined the military. World War II had ended by this point, but it had only been roughly a decade, so there was still strong support for the military. Ross opted to join the Air Force and stayed in Florida at first. Yet, after a few years, he was sent to the one place in the country that was the polar opposite of his home state: Alaska. There are a lot of animals in this state, but there aren't many people. It also provided him with an entirely new perspective on the world around him.

Bob's fascination with art began at a young age. His mother, who would draw and paint with him, inspired him. Bob would spend hours sketching and drawing, and his mother would frequently display his work in their home. Bob grew older and began to take his art more seriously, seeking out opportunities to improve his talents.

Robert entered the United States Air Force at the age of 18 and was stationed in Alaska. During his time there, he developed an interest in painting and enrolled in art lessons at a nearby hobby shop. He also became acquainted with the work of Bill Alexander, a German painter who taught a wet-on-wet painting method that became a trademark of Bob's own style.

Bob followed a career in art after leaving the military in 1960. He trained with Alexander and eventually worked as a traveling salesperson for Bill Alexander's Magic White, Alexander's art supplies company. Bob established his own distinct painting style during this time, emphasizing strong colors, basic shapes, and a free, impressionistic technique.

Bill Alexander was a German painter who created a wet-on-wet painting technique that allowed painters to finish paintings quickly. This technique involved the use of "magic white," an unique white oil paint that allowed colors to merge seamlessly on the canvas. Alexander's technique quickly gained popularity among painters, and he finally established his own art supply firm to market and sell his items.

In the early 1960s, Bob Ross joined Alexander's organization as a traveling salesperson and instructor. He toured the country selling art supplies and exhibiting Alexander's wet-on-wet technique. Bob immediately established a reputation as a gifted and engaging educator, and his demonstrations drew big crowds of eager artists.

During his tenure with Alexander's company, Bob Ross created his own distinct painting style, which combined parts of Alexander's technique with his own personal touches. Bob's paintings emphasized the beauty of nature with vibrant colors, simple shapes, and a loose, impressionistic style.

Bob's time as a traveling salesperson for Alexander's company helped shape his career as an artist and instructor. He improved his teaching abilities while also learning more about the art world and the demands of aspiring artists. His time on the road also allowed him to travel to different parts of the country and meet individuals from various backgrounds.

Bob began teaching painting classes in Florida in the late 1970s. Around this time, he created the notion for "The Joy of Painting," a show that would go on to become his most famous work. The show featured Bob teaching viewers his wet-on-wet painting technique in a calm and encouraging setting. Because of the show's popularity, Bob became a beloved figure in popular culture and an inspiration to young artists all around the world.

Because his personal life was kept confidential, it is possible to rapidly get over the larger elements that are not normally presented on the show. He married his first wife shortly after joining the service. They had two kids during their marriage, one of whom became a painter and occasionally appeared on the show with his father. He divorced his first wife in 1981 and married his second wife from Alaska. They had a son together who also became an artist. His second wife died from cancer in 1993. Ross did not remarry and died before his second wife. Some accounts claim he remarried before his death, but Ross was able to keep most of his personal life hidden from the public eye, so it's unknown. Given how much he shared with his audience, he kept what he didn't share to himself.

Chapter 2:
The Military

"Talent is a pursued interest. Anything that you're willing to practice, you can do."

One of the things that most people don't know about Bob Ross is that he served in the military. With his placid demeanor, it's impossible to imagine the painter carrying a gun or engaging in potentially violent behavior. However, he enlisted in the Air Force. Ross was not sent to any wars, thus he was not put in scenarios typical of military members (most people who serve do not get sent into action). Nonetheless, he did wind up in a predicament that most people will find difficult to reconcile with his reputation. His military career began quietly, with him stationed near his hometown. Yet, like most military personnel, this did not last long, and when he was posted somewhere fresh, it was as far away from home as possible.

Ross entered the Air Force in 1961, after the Korean War but before the Vietnam War began. He was sent to Alaska, where he spent the most of his 20-year military career at Eielson Air Force Base's base clinic. He spent the majority of his military career living as far away from Florida's beaches and moderate climates as feasible. It was the first time he had seen snow, which was a huge change because it wasn't a modest amount. Ross went from never having lived in a frigid environment to living in a state that gets more snow than any other in the country. He was also used to the flat, sandy soils that allowed him to see for kilometers into the distance. Alaska boasts some of the largest mountains in the country, and they conceal behind clouds and snow so that each day is different. There are even days when it's easy to forget about the mountains since they've been shrouded in the clouds for months.

It's easy to understand how much of a visual shock this must have been for someone coming from a flat, warm region; how it must have felt like a whole different world. And this impression is reflected in his work. Several of the landscapes he painted over the years include mountains rising over evergreen trees native to North America's west coast. Snow appears frequently in his photographs.

He had a career that became increasingly dissimilar to the kind-hearted person he was against this wonderfully gorgeous backdrop. Finally, he advanced to the rank of military training teacher, also known as a drill sergeant to civilians. "I was the guy who makes you scrub the toilet, the one who makes you make your bed, the man who screams at you for being late to work," Ross later explained, "and I was fed up with it. I told myself that if I ever got away from it, it wasn't going to be that way again."

Ross' military service shaped him into someone he wasn't, but it also inspired him to become the most-watched artist of all time. His soothing voice was exactly what lulled viewers into watching his show, despite the fact that many of them had no interest in painting themselves. Possessing a presence that generated such a warm, safe environment gave him the kind of broad appeal that has kept him popular decades after his death. Many listened to him online as the Internet (which was not widely available when he died) grew in popularity because he gave a peaceful tone and hypnotic brush strokes. Even his future career began while he was in Alaska - this is where he eventually began painting.

Chapter 3:
Alaska

"We artists are a different breed of people. We're a happy bunch."

Because most people cannot live there, one of the factors that makes love for Alaska comprehensible is the state's breathtaking beauty. Of doubt, the snow contributes to Alaska's beauty, but the mountains and largely natural surroundings have a universal appeal, even if viewed from the comfort of a cabin or lobby. Outside of the Earth's highest latitudes, it is uncommon to find glaciers and wide swaths of land. The harsh, unforgiving environment possesses unequaled beauty and is ideal for inspiring artists.

Ross enrolled in various painting classes while at the base. Any initial excitement he may have felt seemed to fade quickly, as he later recalled, "They'd tell you what makes a tree, but they wouldn't tell you how to paint a tree." In an attempt to find the kind of instruction he wasn't getting, Ross began to look elsewhere, an action he may have learned from his military service. His first sessions were in the Anchorage USO club, and his opinions frequently differed from those of the instructors. Abstract art was a prominent art genre at the time, which is probably why the instructor spent so much time helping his students improve their talents in painting abstract art. It also explains Ross's frustration: he wanted to paint a tree, not just the notion of a tree or a hint of a tree. Surrounded by such natural beauty, he appeared to want to be able to capture the world he saw because he didn't intend to stay in Alaska indefinitely. With a setting so different from where he had grown up, being able to photograph it would allow him to practically take the images with him.

He was determined not to let it go or muddle through, so he looked for a solution that was conveniently accessible from his Alaskan home. Regrettably, the Internet had yet to be invented and was still several decades away from becoming generally available. He sought assistance in locating an affordable and convenient facility to learn to paint. With significantly fewer alternatives, he began searching for shows on the few available channels. This is when he came upon The Magic of Oil Painting, a painting show hosted by German painter William Alexander. He hosted the show to teach more people a form of art method utilized by artists such as Monet to produce works rapidly. The technique was known as wet-on-wet, and it required no drying time.

Ross began to create his own version of the painting approach after seeing the episode to complete a picture during his 30-minute work breaks. When questioned later, Ross stated, "I developed ways of painting extremely fast. I used to go home at lunch and do a couple while I had my sandwich. I'd take them back that afternoon and sell them." This provided him with a way to relax between having to shout at lower-ranking members of the Air Force, and it also helped to supplement his income. His military service also contributed to his ability to paint rapidly and efficiently.

He discovered a way to change occupations after 20 years in the service. Given how long he had been in the service, he could retire rather than simply leave. Because of the number of paintings he could sell, this enabled him to retire. He did not, however, begin by painting on canvas. His initial works were on gold pots, the bottoms of which he painted. These he sold for around $25, a much bigger figure at the time than it is now. He subsequently went on to canvases, which he sold for much more money despite the fact that he had completed them during his sabbatical. This was certainly a cause for his audience to purchase the painting, given he completed it in such a short amount of time. As his earnings from his painting exceeded his earnings from the Air Force, Ross decided it was time to quit the military and pursue a job that he was passionate about. Ross left the Air Force and took on what most people would consider a dream career in 1981, the same year he divorced his first wife. His next part was as William Alexander's apprentice, the man who hosted The Magic of Oil Painting.

Chapter 4:
Method and Mentor

"Gotta give him a friend. Like I always say,
'Everyone needs a friend.'"

Ross had previously worked as an art instructor before leaving the military to work as an apprentice to a painter on television. Regardless of how instructors have been portrayed, his role as a drill sergeant was not helpful in mentoring individuals in art. There have been some harsh educators, but most work is best done when instructors encourage students rather than sharply criticize and condescend, an idea that Ross grasped without difficulty. After clashing with his own instructors at the USO club, he began teaching at Eielson Air Force Base. He began teaching others his adopted style, assisting them in learning how to enjoy painting the beautiful nature surrounding them. At one of his sessions, he and the small class were taken, with the caption resembling the description of his show.

BRUSHMAN - MSgt. Bob Ross, first sergeant of the USAF Clinic, completes one of three Alaskan nature images he painted at a recent art display for employees and retired residents of the Pioneers Homes in Fairbanks, Alaska. Sergeant Ross presented the paintings to the elderly home after the protest.

Much of the image is quite familiar because it is typical of what you might see on one of his performances, with two noticeable exceptions. The first was that the shot was taken with the audience in mind, placing Ross at the rear rather than the front. The second feature is his hair. It depicts Ross's naturally straight hair, like in most of his military photographs. He hadn't yet developed his unique look. Instead, he resembled a well-groomed military man, which took a lot more money to maintain because it required frequent haircuts. The Magic of Oil Painting premiered in 1974, just a few years after Ross began painting. Ross learned a lot about how to speed up the process after observing Alexander use the wet-on-wet technique (previously known as alla prima). This procedure allows you to use oil paints on oil paints that have not yet dried. Because oil paintings can take a long time to dry, more traditional methods require painters to wait for one layer to dry before moving on to the next. Furthermore, the approach necessitates a thinner upper layer to avoid mixing or altering the bottom layers. If you've seen one of

Ross's exhibitions, you'll know that he constantly dips his brush in a solution to clean it, which also ensures a thinner paint layer. He then removes the majority of the liquid by slapping the brush against his easel in a repetitive and loud manner. Listening to it, the sound of the brush drying on the easel is louder than Ross's voice. After cleaning and drying, the next color is added, keeping the new paint as light as possible. This is accomplished by applying less pressure and touching the canvas gently.

Because oil paints can take up to a week to cure, this technique has traditionally taken longer. Artists developed a method of painting swiftly without having to wait hours or days for a layer to dry by being careful with the application and amount of paint used. It was utilized by the Impressionists, and it is ideal for landscapes because there is less need to capture every detail. Unfortunately, it is not suitable for paintings such as portraits and close-up photos, which require more accurate strokes. You can hear how the brush reacts with the canvas when you watch Ross. The larger, wider brushes are often employed at the start to finish the base layer, which gives you the sky, water, and landscape. The mountains are then painted, with the paint being thicker than in most other regions. If you pay carefully, you'll see that in the next few minutes of painting, he avoids the mountains, allowing them to dry as he works on other portions of the canvas. Following that, more delicate brushes are employed, and while you can hear how hard he pushes on the canvas, it is quite targeted, like when adding the trees. When you watch an episode, you'll see how the first layer is worked into the canvas so it doesn't smear or mix with later paints. This is the style that Alexander utilized, and Ross mastered it while in the service, completing many portraits per day while working a full-time job.

Ross began to collaborate with his master, Alexander, even borrowing one of Alexander's slogans, "happy little trees," to make painting feel more approachable. Because painting had been such a blessing to him growing up in Germany, Alexander believed that everyone should be able to paint. Most of the environment he witnessed as a child in Germany during World War I reminded him of conflict. He described the scene around him in his book as "killed cows and machine guns bared and laying around, and skeletons of soldiers half-buried with the boots coming out of the earth." To escape the horrors, he would spend time in nature. Alexander was intrigued to see a traveling artist at work when he passed through the neighborhood. He stated that the man's talent was not very noteworthy, but the speed with which he did the work was spectacular. Alexander worked as his apprentice on both landscapes and portraits. With World War II on the horizon, Alexander found himself in the German Army. He was outgoing, and as soldiers learned of his talent, he was frequently asked to create images. During the war, he was kidnapped by Americans, who also put him to work painting in a studio they provided him with. After the war, he moved to Canada, the United States' northern neighbor. Despite his life was not wealthy, he followed in the footsteps of the artists he had seen when he was younger. He and his wife toured North America, mostly in the west. They painted in various spots while touring in their Volkswagen bus.

He came to Los Angeles, where he could finally establish a more permanent residence. Many in the neighborhood admired his flair and commitment. His supporters admired his efforts to make painting more accessible to them. It wasn't long before Ross became one of his students, looking for a chance to hone the skills he'd learned in the military. After attending a lesson, Ross decided that this was the only method of painting that piqued his interest. Alexander was upbeat and encouraging, which was evident in his protégé as well. Their methods of encouragement, however, were completely different. Whereas Ross's encouragement is soothing and almost therapeutic, Alexander's is far more passionate and fiery. Alexander, like Ross later, made up stories as he painted, once asking his audience, "Do you know the trees are listening to you? I truly have learnt that! Wonderful!" His excitement and love for painting were always obvious and apparent, as he knew exactly how it might aid during difficult times. It was both an escape and a means of production.

Ross filled in for Alexander in lessons for several years, educating the pupils with his now-familiar face and tone. This ultimately drew the attention, or perhaps more appropriately, the ear of someone who believed Ross should work independently.

Chapter 5:
From Pupil To Host

"In painting, you have unlimited power. You have the ability to move mountains. You can bend rivers. But when I get home, the only thing I have power over is the garbage."

Ross was able to swiftly adopt and employ aspects of Alexander's methods of inspiring his students, but he maintained his own calm demeanor when speaking to the class. While Alexander was animated and energetic, almost shouting to get his point over, Ross's voice never seemed to rise above the level of a whisper. It didn't take long for Alexander to recognize Ross's talent and recognize how effortlessly he could function as a top pupil. This was Ross's first opportunity to make a living as a painter. Yet, regrettably, he ran into the same issue as Alexander did: it didn't cover his bills as well as he had hoped. Part of the problem was that the cost of living in California was greater, so even though he earned more than he had in the military, he was no longer living in a place where that would go very far.

Frequent haircuts became prohibitively expensive during this period. Attempting to keep his hair at the same length cost him money that could have been spent elsewhere. As a result, he let his hair grow out before getting it permed. The perm curled his hair, making it significantly simpler to go without a haircut for extended periods of time. The issue was that Ross didn't care for the hairdo. And, according to some, he despised his hair. Some assume that the intention was for him to resume his more conventional haircuts once he was financially secure. By the time that happened, it was clear that it was an important part of what made him so distinctive, so he opted to maintain it - especially because it was part of his emblem.

Ross had returned to Florida after working for Alexander and had not left the state since.

As he was teaching for Alexander one day in 1981, someone in the audience wanted to meet the show's star. Annette Kowalski said that she was sad that Alexander would not be the major draw for the studio when it became evident that he would not be teaching. Then Bob Ross began to talk, and the class moved forward, and Kowalski became engrossed in the calming tone and gentle encouragement. She had recently lost a kid at the time, and listening to Ross appeared to help her feel a lot more at ease (something that many people have felt since then). It was like she was getting a little break from everything else. At the end of class, she was ready to approach him about something much bigger: she wanted to be his partner and follow in Alexander's footsteps so that Ross could establish himself. They developed a collaboration, with Ross set to host his own show, and they worked together to generate promotional deals for art materials. Alexander was broadcast on PBS, but the studio made the majority of its money by selling products, particularly supplies.

There were some noticeable variances, and Ross did not want his photographs to be sold. They came to an agreement, and he soon aired a show that was practically identical to Alexander's on paper. In practice, the two artists' drastically different approaches to expressing ideas caused them to appeal to different audiences. However, because he had traveled throughout Europe and North America, Alexander tended to paint a much broader spectrum of landscapes, so his works spanned from regions reminiscent of the Black Forest to landscapes that appeared to be near deserts. Ross's photographs were mainly inspired by Alaska and the breathtaking landscapes that only those who lived in the hard environment could conceive without a photograph. Even when the two artists painted identical landscapes, the end effects were distinctive. Both men created incredible paintings, but the final pieces frequently revealed their disparate approaches to painting and mentorship.

Chapter 6:
The Joy Of Painting

"Don't forget to tell these special people in your life just how special they are to you."

Ross had already made two significant career changes, so he was no stranger to making significant professional adjustments. But this was something altogether else. He was about to do something that would completely alter his and his family's existence. Ross's presentation, which was inspired by his mentor's show, was dubbed The Pleasure of Painting, another thing he and his master had in common. They had discovered painting as a method to temporarily escape from life, and they both believed that art should not be regarded as something unreachable to the majority of people. The way a brush glides across a canvas to create something fresh and fascinating is therapeutic and peaceful, a welcome change from everyday life.

When Ross's show debuted in 1983, the artist was just as encouraging as Alexander, but this time it was a gentle encouragement that struck a particular chord with viewers. Others, like Kowalski, were drawn to the calming directions and positive outlook he gave with each new feature he added to the painting. The viewer watched as a blank canvas was transformed into a beautiful landscape, usually with snow and breathtaking mountains, in less than 30 minutes.

The exhibition appeared to be effortless, as if Ross didn't have to struggle to keep the audience engaged while designing something that could easily hang in any living room, dining room, or corridor. But, Ross's approach to establishing his show was far from effortless. As Kowalski would later remark, he was in charge of everything, aiming for a magnificent spectacle by planning as much as possible. He'd stay up late thinking about the best way to frame things, practicing sentences in his head to urge viewers to feel empowered to paint. Though he avoided raising his voice, Ross was said to be a perfectionist, thus he used his military background to run a very tight ship, tight ship, with others claiming he worked in a precise and demanding manner. He asked no more of the people who worked on the show than he demanded of himself. Managing many aspects of the show, he wanted to ensure a consistent aesthetic with each show, right down to the lighting. Because most palettes throw a shimmer or shine, he took the time to sand down the palettes he used on TV so that his audience was not subjected to the glare of bright lighting on a plastic palette. He adjusted his body and held the palette in such a way that his missing fingertip was hidden. Nothing was overlooked when preparing for the exhibitions, from the lighting to the words he said to the way he advertised art objects.

But one of the things he was most precise about was the types of products he sold. Painting is notoriously expensive, from the paints and canvases that must be refilled on a regular basis to the easel, brushes, and palettes, which are typically highly expensive because they are rarely purchased more than once or twice. Ross sought ways to cut prices so that his audience would not have to spend a fortune to begin painting. He also realized that buying the materials could be difficult because there are so many various paint brands, brush types, and cleaning solutions. To ensure that people could reuse supplies they had already purchased, he created images that were remarkably similar so that his audience could use the same brushes - and, more critically, the same pigments - when they sat down. They would have a much better comprehension of the colors after a few shows, making them more confident when they began painting. He provided solutions to problems such as the cleaner solution, mentioning cleaning chemicals that would help and suggested items that might be used as palettes so that viewers who were concerned about the expense would be more likely to look into purchasing supplies. Instead of purchasing pricey art brushes, he would utilize the types of brushes frequently used to paint a house. This meant that viewers were likely already equipped with some of the necessary brushes. Furthermore, brushes for painting houses are often kept at a reasonable price because most people use them at some point in order to maintain their homes. People routinely purchase these brushes for everything from painting walls to touching up baseboards, so they are designed to be affordable to everyone - something Ross encouraged. The viewer did not have to spend a lot of money on the brushes. All they had to do was go to a home improvement store and get a few brushes that they could also use to touch up their dwellings. Ross also used a standard paint scraper for his paint knife, which saved money because it was not customized. Still, it worked excellent for picking up a few colors and blending them together, or for adding sharper edges, such as the tops of mountains or the trunks of enormous trees. He decreased the cost for viewers to get started by using basic products that they were likely to have around the house.

"The Pleasure of Painting" has evolved into more than just a television show throughout the years. Bob Ross's soothing voice and cheerful attitude have captured the hearts of people from all walks of life, making it a cultural phenomenon and an online meme.

One of the reasons "The Pleasure of Painting" has grown so popular is its ease of access. Bob Ross's style of painting was plain and simple, making it simple for spectators to follow along and produce their own artwork. The show's emphasis on relaxation and positivism also struck a chord with viewers, who found it to be a welcome diversion from the stresses of everyday life.
Another factor contributing to the show's longevity is its capacity to bring people together. Fans of "The Joy of Painting" have formed online communities and social media groups to share their artwork and communicate with other admirers. The show has also spawned a slew of parodies and tributes, including a popular YouTube channel dedicated to edited versions of the show set to music.

Because the aim of the show was for viewers to be able to paint while Ross painted, the show was designed to be mostly in real-time, albeit not live. They would occasionally make cuts, removing bloopers or other minor issues. For example, Ross would occasionally apply too much pressure, knocking down the easel. This type of thing was taken out of the show. Otherwise, his flaws on the canvas were left in so that he could demonstrate how any variation or divergence may be a "happy little accident" that could be transformed into a stunning contribution. The version of the artwork he created for the event was not the first of its kind. The benefit of the wet-on-wet process was that it allowed you to finish a painting rapidly, which Ross took use of to refine his images before the presentation. Ross developed a landscape to use as a reference when painting on air for the first time. His on-air image was the second iteration of a painting he created. There was also a third version, which took him longer to produce and was included in his art displays and books. These were the versions that were shown as the official version. Every work he painted on the spot had two variations, indicating that he was a prolific painter.

The show went on to become a huge success. For the second season, there would be a ceremonial brush change as Alexander transferred the painting torch to Ross. It was a wonderful method for them to demonstrate that they did not see each other as competitors. But, that was not a sentiment that would persist.

Bob Ross was well-known for his distinct painting style, which stressed simplicity, innovation, and optimism. His wet-on-wet technique and the concept of "happy accidents" have become synonymous with his style, inspiring many painters worldwide.

Wet-on-wet painting is a method in which wet paint is applied to wet paint, allowing colors to merge and form soft, flowing designs. William Alexander pioneered this technique, but Bob Ross established his own distinct style by creating a smooth foundation layer on the canvas with a special white oil paint known as "magic white." He would then paint over this basic layer with a variety of brushes and tools to add texture and detail.

The concept of "happy accidents" is one of the most well-known features of Bob Ross's approach to painting. This term alludes to the unanticipated outcomes that can occur during the painting process, such as a stray brushstroke or a paint smear. Instead of viewing these failures as mistakes, Bob Ross saw them as opportunities to be creative and experiment. He would frequently incorporate these blunders into new components of his paintings, employing them to add depth, texture, and interest.

Bob Ross' approach to painting was based on his art and life philosophy. He thought that anyone, regardless of ability level or background, could learn to paint. He also believed that painting may help people connect with their emotions and achieve calm and relaxation as a therapeutic and contemplative exercise. His shows frequently carried messages of hope and encouragement, and he would frequently close each episode with the phrase "happy painting, and God bless."

Chapter 7:
Beyond The Camera

"Use absolutely no pressure. Just like an angel's wing."

Ross had more than just his show and art supplies. He began publishing books pretty early in his television career. They were crucial in getting his art out there, especially in the early days of his art supply. He was willing to sell art objects that complemented the show, but by the time he was on the air, Ross no longer seemed interested in selling his photographs. Instead of selling them, he would occasionally give them away for charity auctions. Otherwise, the works would be stored by Bob Ross Inc., the firm that would supply his art supplies.

Ross was a huge success from the start of his new career. Over the years, his company would be worth $15 million, which was incredible for something that began as a PBS broadcast. The event was essentially a means for him to advertise the rest of what he sold, however he dedicated more time to it and the premise that everyone could paint.

He, like Alexander, taught his students, though this was significantly less accessible to the majority of people. An individual session with Ross might be had for $374 per hour. Even still, it was something that only a few people would be able to do. The painter also paid attention to his students, assessing their ability to see who could go on to teach, just as he had. Individuals who demonstrated exceptional skill could work as Bob Ross-certified instructors. As people began to gather to observe him, his former students began to launch businesses as instructors, teaching the approach to individuals at a much lesser charge than Ross himself. They also taught their own classes, forming a community of painters who emulated his technique and tried to make the art world more accessible to all. However, not everyone was thrilled to see Ross rise to such prominence. Ross had become far more important and well-known than Alexander, the guy who had accepted him as a student. When Ross initially started, Alexander Arts was enormously popular, owing to the premise that paintings could be produced in under 30 minutes (something that Alexander did before Ross). Alexander would go on to voice feelings of betrayal, believing that not only did Ross take his painting method, but that Ross believed he could do it better. It wasn't Alexander's method, but one that had been in place long before he was born. He'd made alterations to accommodate touring and painting rather than putting it into a show. Ross tweaked the style even more, although the painting approach diverged from what Ross had learned from Alexander. Alexander's business approach was mainly imitated by Ross. The format of The Pleasure of Painting, several of his expressions, and approach to encouraging were all quite similar. Because there is no reason to reinvent the wheel when something works, business models are frequently replicated. The phrases Ross inherited from his master were not initially an issue, but rather an extension of Alexander's approach to painting. He had encouraged Ross in the early days of The Pleasure of Painting, but his own expressions were identified with Ross rather than him over time. Ross's brand and legacy quickly became mainstream, whereas Alexander's business had reached a stalemate.

While Alexander gave Ross a lot of his start in art, what he presented to the audience was radically different from what Alexander offered. Alexander was energetic and feisty, his voice increasing at times due to his German accent. He was upbeat and encouraging, which was ideal for many who had previously perceived art as solemn and depressing. He told them they could be artists and demonstrated how simple it was, including their thinking. Ross approached the same model with many of the same principles from a peaceful, relaxing perspective. This attracts not only people interested in painting and art, but also people looking to unwind at the end of the day. They would watch not to learn how to paint (many of his viewers had no desire to take up a brush), but to see this upbeat man make something they would be glad to buy for their homes. Ross offered a terrific method to unwind and relax after work or school; he was a calming presence that people looked to for enjoyment. The difference was in the presentation; Ross appealed to his audience since just listening to him made them feel better. Some people who had watched the show for a few years to unwind would be motivated to try painting over time, but they didn't have to. Whereas Alexander might motivate people to try, Ross motivated them to unwind and enjoy themselves. They both had their own charms and ways of encouraging people, but it was Ross's folksy, mellow delivery that truly struck a chord with American listeners.

It didn't hurt that Ross was instantly identifiable, thanks in large part to his hair. It had an unusual appearance (and remains fairly uncommon on TV). When individuals switched channels, his presence drew people's attention before the volume adjusted (back in the day, images tended to appear before the sound, so it was possible to flip through channels without hearing anything other than the white noise, but the images were relatively clear as soon as you changed the channel). The hairdo, which was intended to save money, became part of the legend and helped him stand out. Ross stood out among those affiliated with the art scene.

He wore flannels and trousers with his large hair, and he had a lot of facial hair that suited his hair. As a result, he resembled everyone else, making him feel more like an instructor at a local public painting class than someone on TV. Ross's appearance also made satire and cosplay much easier. A person does not need a large budget to look like Ross; just enough for hair and makeup.

Chapter 8:
His Own Style

"You can have anything you want in the world — once you help everyone around you get what they want."

Ross did more than just paint on his show, and he wasn't the only person who appeared on the screen. The painter invited one of his sons to the show in Episode 13 of his first season, and instead of painting, they held a question-and-answer session. This demonstrates not only how distinct the show was from the norm, but also how forward-thinking he was. Ross's technique was much more like to today's vlogs and streams, in which he attempted to communicate with his viewers as much as possible. That wasn't possible in real time, but he devised a method of interaction that was significantly more entertaining than most other shows at the time. In the episode, his son sits next him, evidently still very little and resembling his father minus the long hair. They had gone through the multitude of questions that people had asked - Ross had made a tremendous impression in only 12 episodes - and were answering the most frequently requested queries (before the term FAQ was in common use). Ross then pledged to answer questions on a more personal level for folks whose inquiries were not as often asked, therefore they were left out of the broadcast.

His kid posed the questions, and Ross responded. Ross had a painting and an easel nearby to explain the answers to the questions. In this episode, he was far more like a teacher and far less like the serene artist from the previous shows, indicating what he was like in the more private lessons. While he remains cool, his statements have more emphasis and repetition to clarify and drive home ideas in response to the inquiries. For example, when one of the queries was about brushes, he gave advice on where to get them and what to look for. It's a change, yet nothing has changed from the previous programs' persona. The show is akin to watching content creators nowadays in that they deliver considerably more in-depth responses to inquiries. Ross began to regard his instructor as a competition at some point, expressing a similar viewpoint to the New York Times in 1991. This is possibly what made Alexander feel betrayed. Artists have always had a complicated relationship with their mentors, with some being extremely supportive and others being cynical or jealous. Alexander was delighted with Ross' success until Ross stated that he saw his mentor as a competition, which is why he didn't discuss Alexander's company on his show. Both had suffered in the creative industry, despite coming from quite different backgrounds and having different reasons for desiring an outlet to relax. They did, however, share similar artistic ambitions and concepts. How open they believed it should be to all. Over time, the business became a source of contention, resulting in a schism that would not have arisen otherwise. It also demonstrates a shift in Ross, who was previously Alexander's student and instructor. Yet, this is to be expected. Students learn and improve as they create their own work and process. Nevertheless, most of their philosophies were extremely similar.

Ross' approach to painting was to make art extremely approachable, which he accomplished by talking and directing his audience. In his concerts, he always emphasizes talent level because he wants everyone to believe they can achieve it. Yet, it has been simple to select images to emphasize where people should start if they wish to focus on a skill level. This is now simple, with a fast online search yielding numerous ideas for photographs suitable for novices. There are also articles and blogs regarding what may be learned from specific images and episodes. Many of the concepts are inspired by something he stated on the show. Some, on the other hand, are dependent on the amount of effort put into each image, such as having less color mixing or fewer items to cover.

Despite having three copies of a painting, Ross never seemed to want others to feel obligated to create a painting that was identical to his. Instead, he wanted them to be distinctive, to demonstrate their individuality as artists. That's why he talked of inhabiting the paintings he created. It is easier to think about what you want to add to make it your own if you imagine yourself living in the photos. The audience gets the impression from the way he speaks that they can not only paint but also make their own improvements.

Ross continued to work until the year he died. Notwithstanding the difficulties, he lived as discreetly as possible in the suburbs with his family. He was unaffected by his popularity, largely acting the same onscreen as he would offscreen. Audiences didn't see how much time and work went into the show, nor how much he tried to ensure that each show ran smoothly and easily. But the man they envisaged from that easy image appeared to be the man he was most of the time when he wasn't in front of the cameras. The fact that two of his sons followed him into art shows how well he motivates others. Ross was diagnosed with late-stage lymphoma in 1994, not long after his second wife died. Interested in getting the offered treatment, Ross had to cease hosting the show because the procedure was rigorous and taxing. His final episode aired on May 17, 1994, and he died a little more than a year later, on July 4, 1995. He was returned to his birthplace, New Smyrna Beach, and buried there.

Chapter 9:
A Legacy

"We don't really know where this goes — and I'm not sure we really care."

Despite certain unpleasant aspects of the profession, Ross has become a legend who has only grown in popularity decades after his death. Much of this is due to how calm his voice and word choices made people feel. He's also become very popular in mainstream culture, with several shows including him with little to no introduction. One of the most intriguing and underappreciated examples of Ross in pop culture comes from the TV show Creepshow and horror anthology with the legendary figure, the Crypt Keeper. Season 2 premiered in 2021 and features a familiar-looking man fighting the Deadites, the adversaries from The Evil Dead. The episode is titled "Public Television of the Dead," and the main character isn't named Bob Ross, but he has the same hair, is a painter, and works on the show's public access station. The show within the show is called The Love of Painting with Norm Roberts, and it bears all of the hallmarks of The Joy of Painting, including Ross's catchphrase at the end of the show, "Happy painting and God bless." Ted Raimi, brother to Sam Raimi (the director behind The Evil Dead), plays one of the characters - the first to become a Deadite. It's an intriguing blend of two prominent 1980s icons, and it's something for fans of Ross and horror. It also gives the Deadites a much quieter tone, making it extremely distinctive and entertaining.

His online presence is far more pervasive. Nonetheless, he had a resurgence of attention even before the pandemic, owing to the fact that he appeared to be operating more like a content creator long before the Internet was ubiquitous. Others portraying him have appeared in several aspects of his online presence, such as Epic Rap Battles of History, in which he faced off against Pablo Picasso, which was released in 2013. A 200-hour marathon hosted on Twitch near the end of 2015 propelled him to fame at the conclusion of the 2010s. The site is known for gaming, but when the marathon to honor Ross aired, over five million people tuned in for hours to listen to him and watch him paint the familiar, magnificent landscapes. Bill Moorier, the Head of Twitch Creative, recognized how much people like watching Ross after the astonishing number of views. Reruns of the show became a frequent occurrence on the platform as a result of his efforts. He was also extremely popular in Europe. By February of the following year, reruns of Ross' show were as popular as the most popular gaming channels, with around 5,000 views per episode. Of course, some spectators created their own entertainment by acting as if the presentation were live and wondering why he was ignoring their questions. It was mostly harmless entertainment, but it did demonstrate how much the younger generation admired a man who died long before they were born - this was the only way they could contact him.

Then came 2020, 25 years after his death, and people all over the world began searching for Ross as they went into lockdown. In 2015, he was introduced to younger generations, making him appear to four generations as the globe looked to turn upside down. They watched his show with the intention of painting because there was nothing else to do. Many who didn't want to paint simply wanted to feel the nostalgia and peace that Ross radiates on his shows. During the course of a quarter-century, he assisted those in need, and it's tough not to assume that he would have been overjoyed to learn that he was assisting so many people.

CONCLUSION

Few celebrities have been as well-known as Bob Ross. Positively inspiring and instantly recognizable. He doesn't elicit the kind of immediate response that many celebrities with large fan bases do. Instead, the very mention of Bob Ross makes people grin and want to watch his show to unwind.

A part of his legacy has been to instill a sense of calm and security through the sounds of his encouraging voice, which was originally intended to reassure people they could paint but has come to be used in a variety of other scenarios. He pushed the message of his mentor that painting isn't something for odd people and stuffy affluent types but an activity for everyone. It's a safe place to go to get away from problems, even only for a little while. It doesn't cost much to get started, nor does it take much time. In 30 minutes, with roughly eight colors, anyone may create a picture they can hang in their home. It may not be flawless, but it is yours. It's a universal message with a far broader meaning. During some particularly trying moments, his broadcast was as much a haven as the activity he promoted. One does not have to be an art specialist to appreciate Bob Ross's work.

We've looked at the life and legacy of Bob Ross, an artist and instructor who won the hearts of millions of people around the world with his unique approach to painting and message of positivity and creativity. Bob Ross's art and life philosophy has influenced innumerable young artists and creatives, and his legacy lives on today.

As we near the end of this book, we invite readers to incorporate Bob Ross's art and life philosophy into their own creative pursuits. Whether you are an accomplished artist or a beginner, Bob Ross' method to painting and his philosophy of positivism and self-expression may teach you a lot.

One of the important messages from this book is the value of simplicity in art. Bob Ross's paintings were distinguished by bright colors, simple shapes, and a loose, impressionistic style that accentuated nature's beauty. Bob Ross was able to make paintings that were both beautiful and approachable by focusing on the essentials and letting go of perfectionism.

Another major takeaway from Bob Ross' painting method is the concept of "happy accidents." Instead of viewing faults as mistakes, Bob Ross saw them as opportunities to be creative and improvise. This frame of mind enabled him to approach his art with a feeling of humor and exploration, resulting in some of his most recognizable paintings.

Ultimately, Bob Ross's art and life philosophy reminds us of the value of positivism and self-expression. We can tap into a sense of inner serenity and contentment that can help many aspects of our lives by embracing our own unique creative voice and finding joy in the process of making art.

THANKS YOU!

Printed in Dunstable, United Kingdom

75320184R00022